My

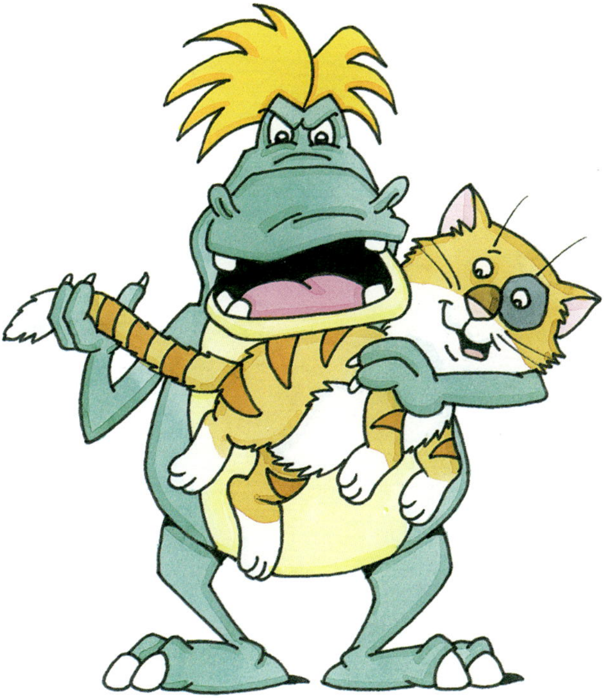

Illustrated by Kelvin Hawley

Rigby

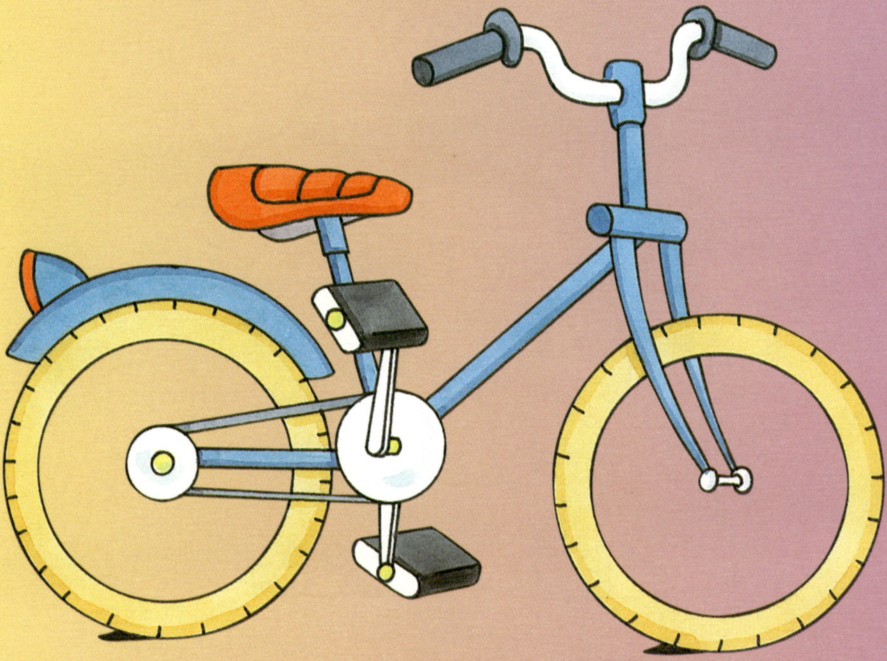

my bike

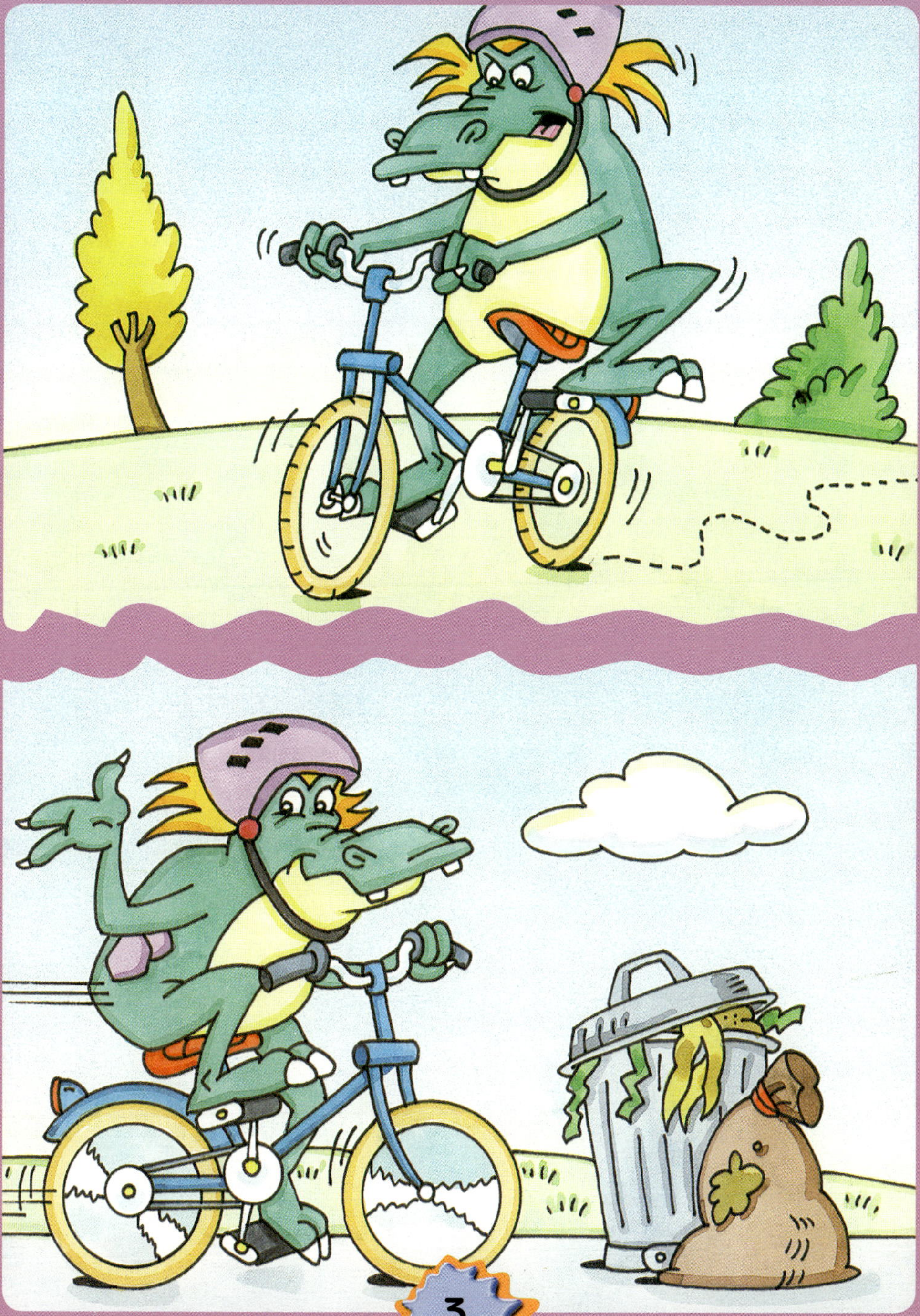

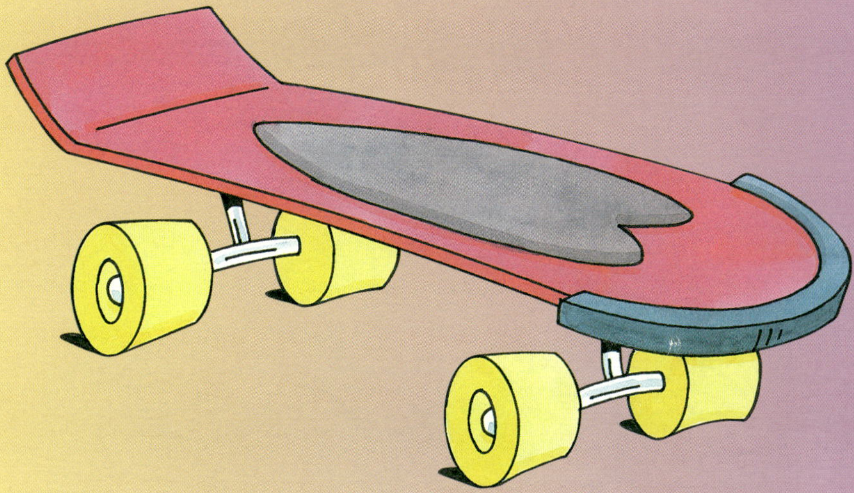

my skateboard

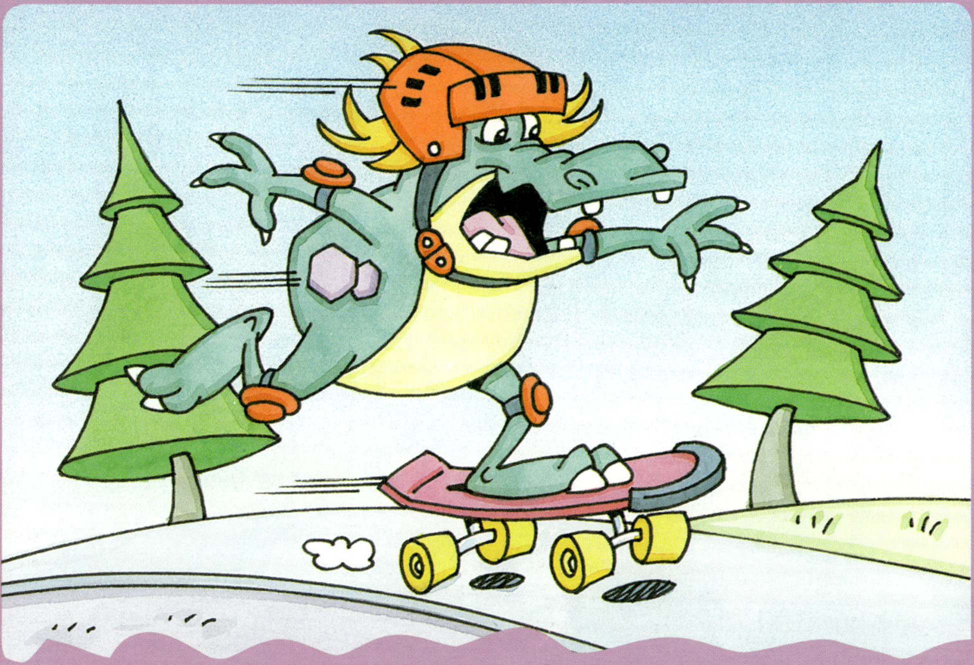

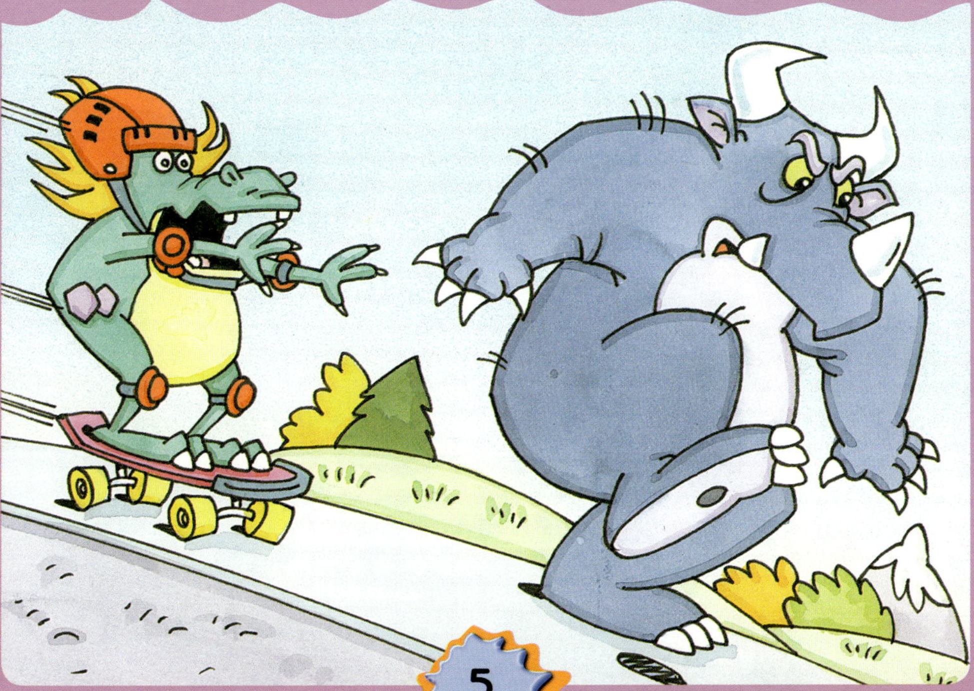

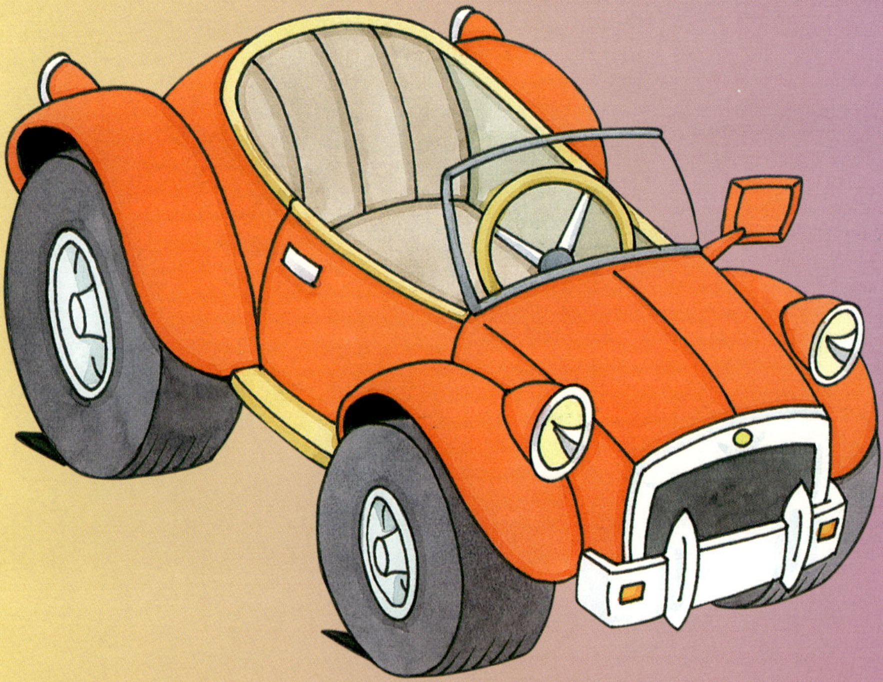

my car

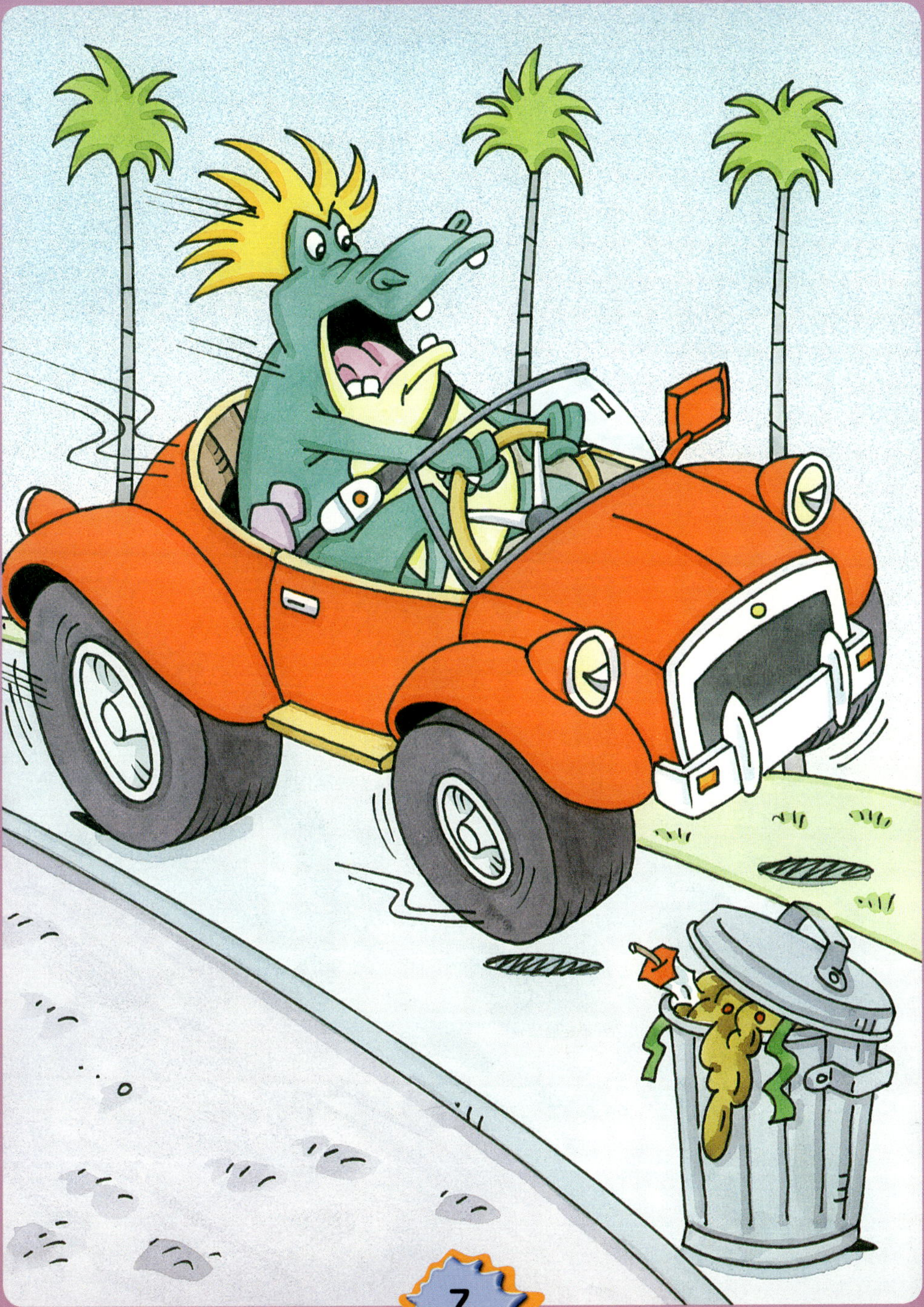

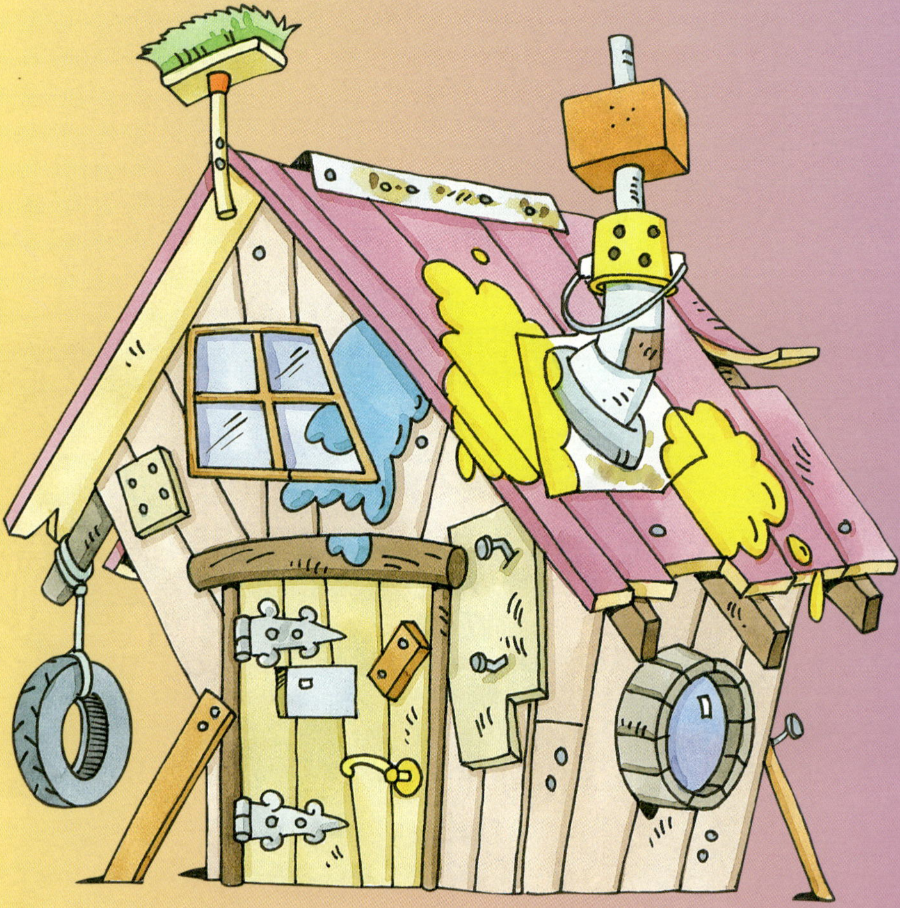

my house

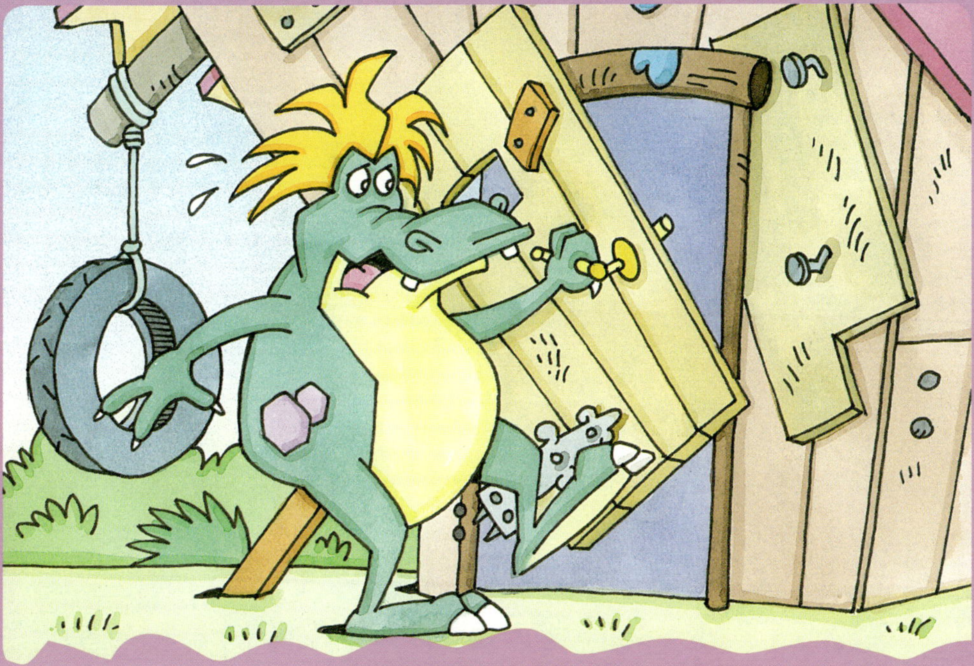

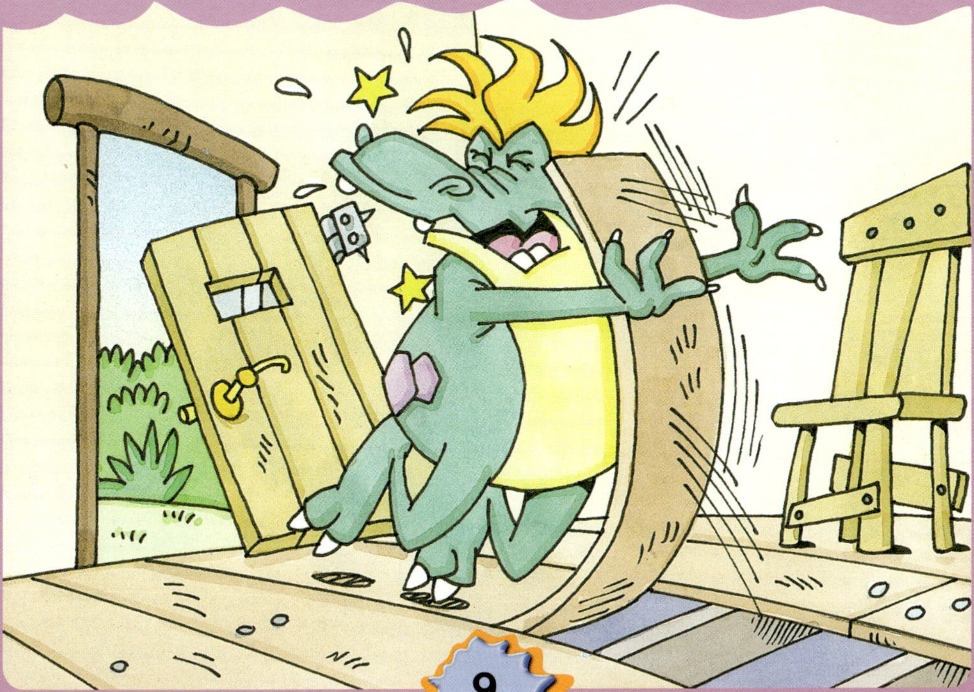

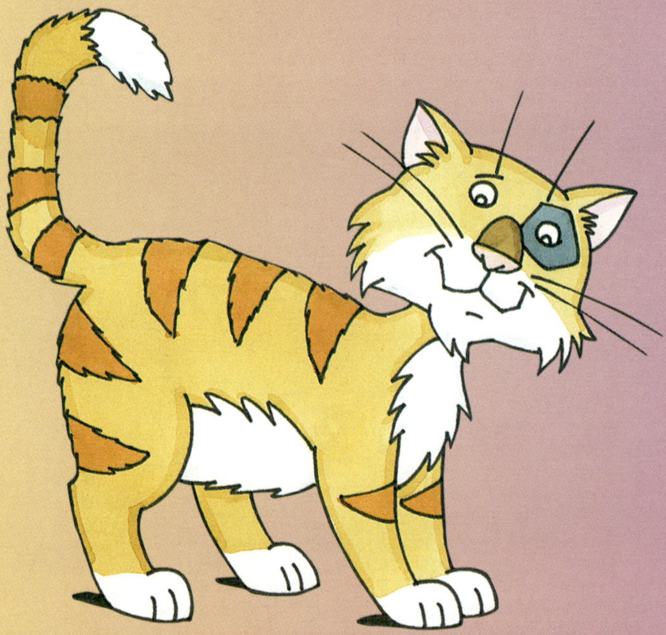

my cat

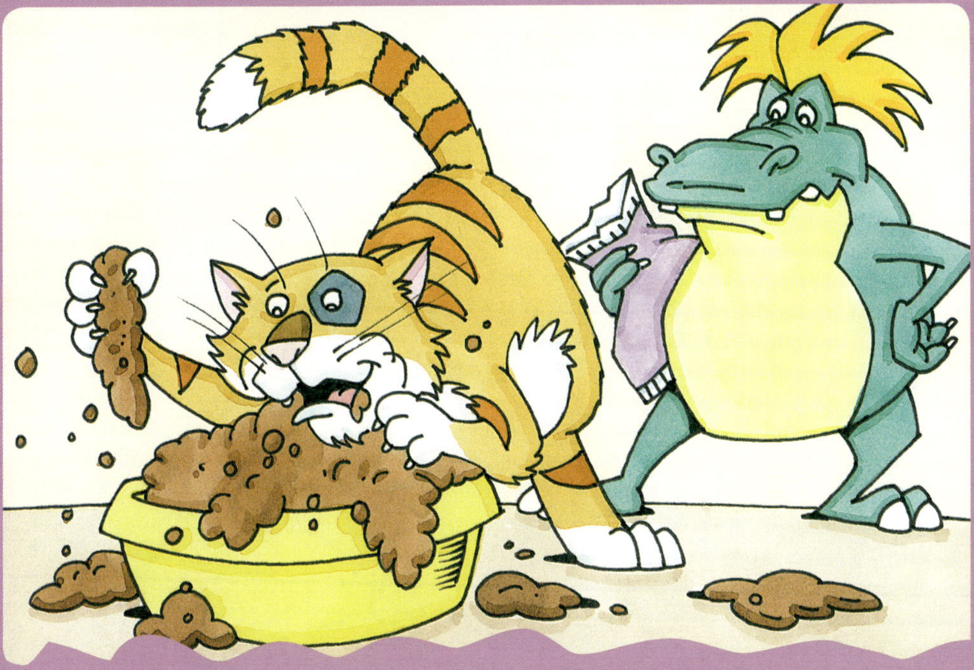

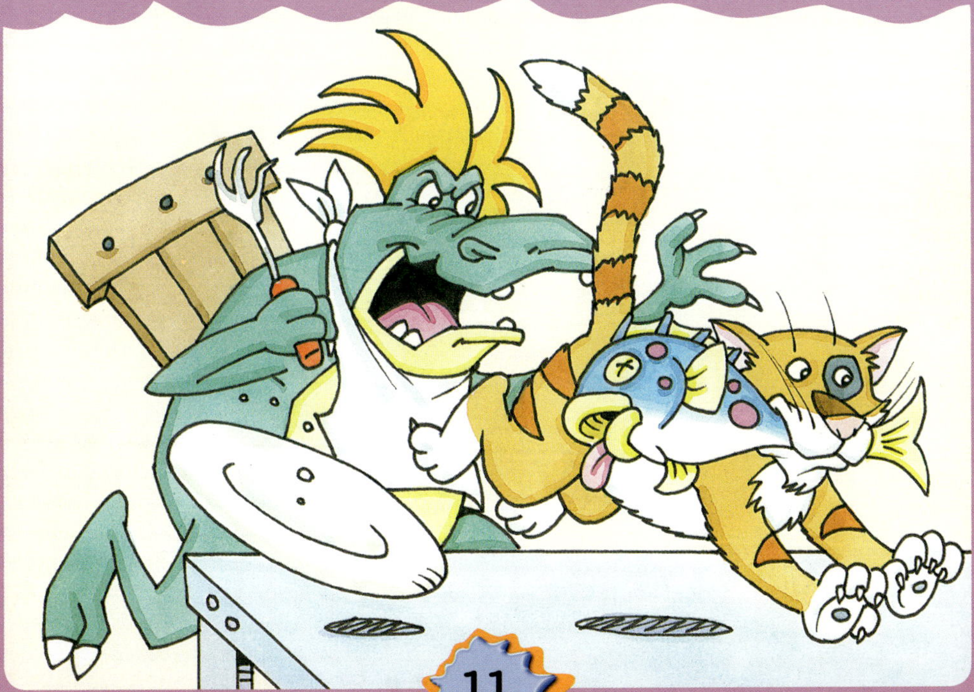

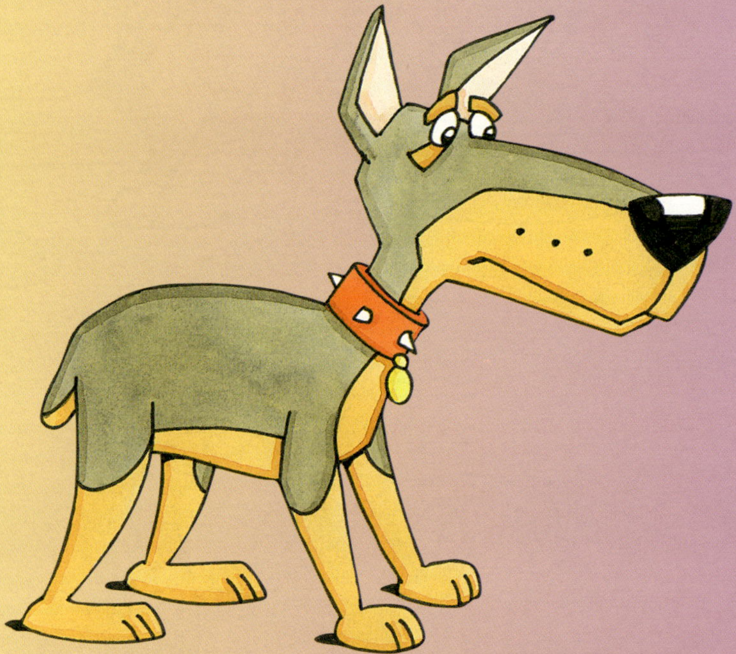

my dog

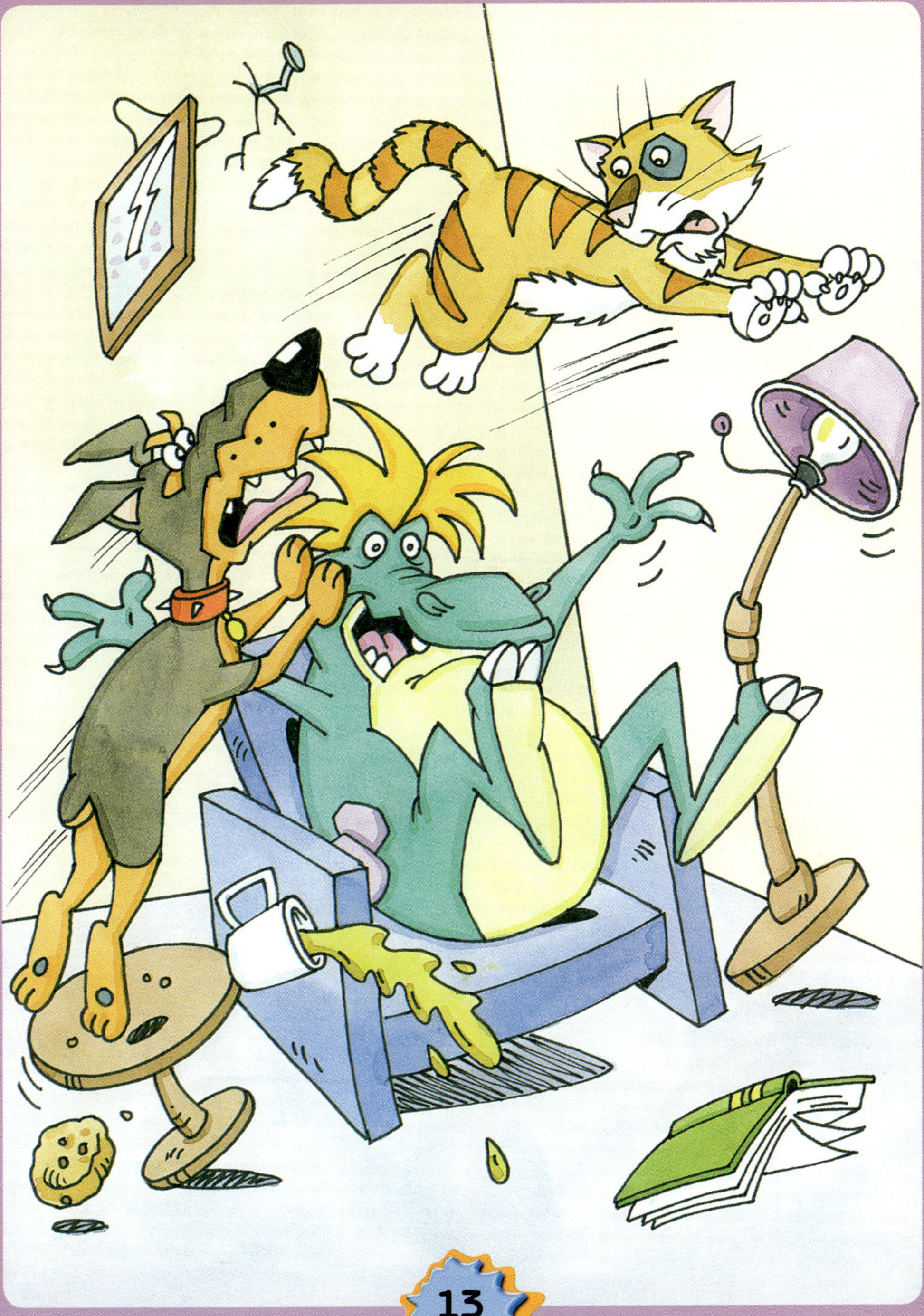

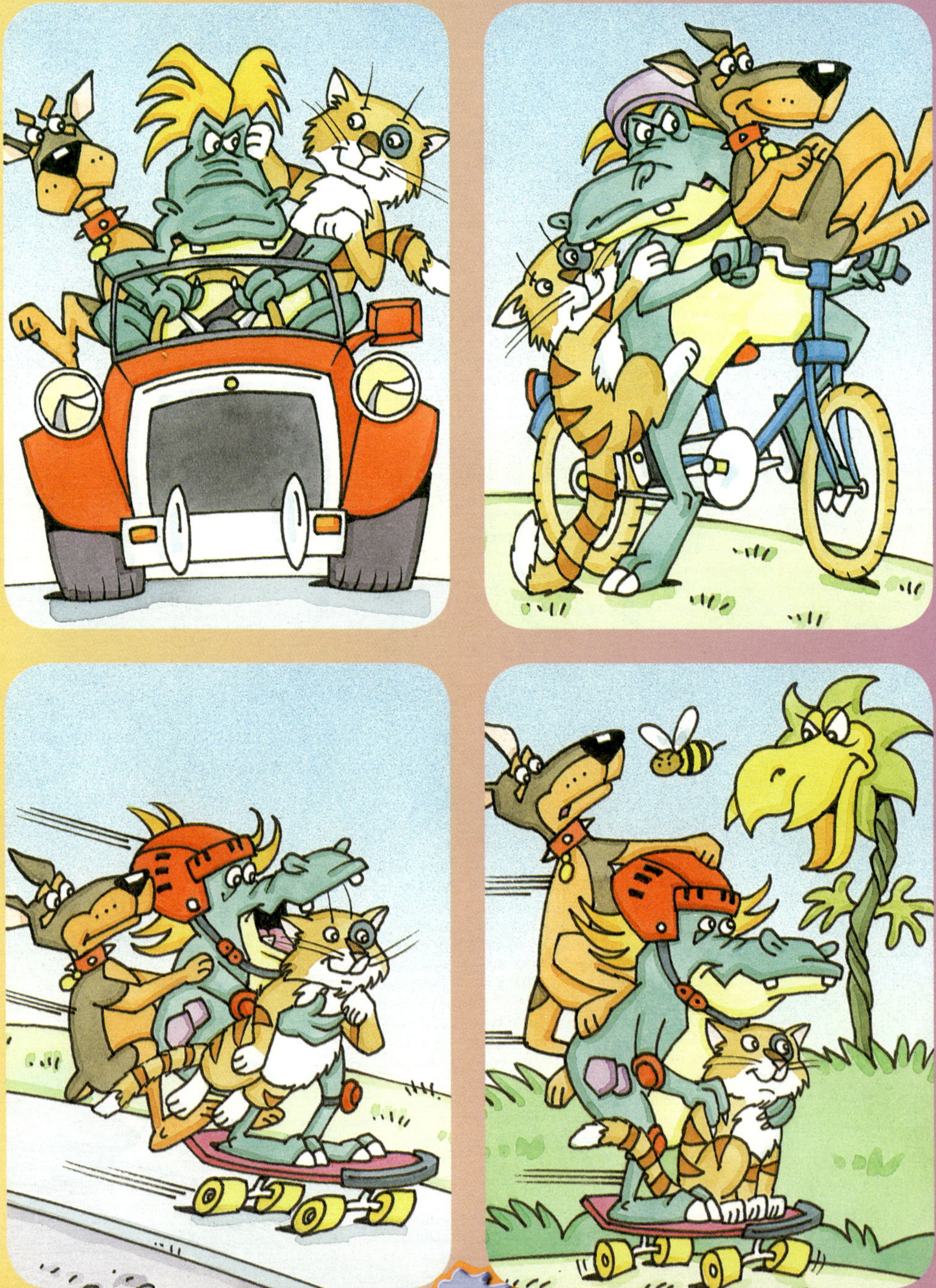

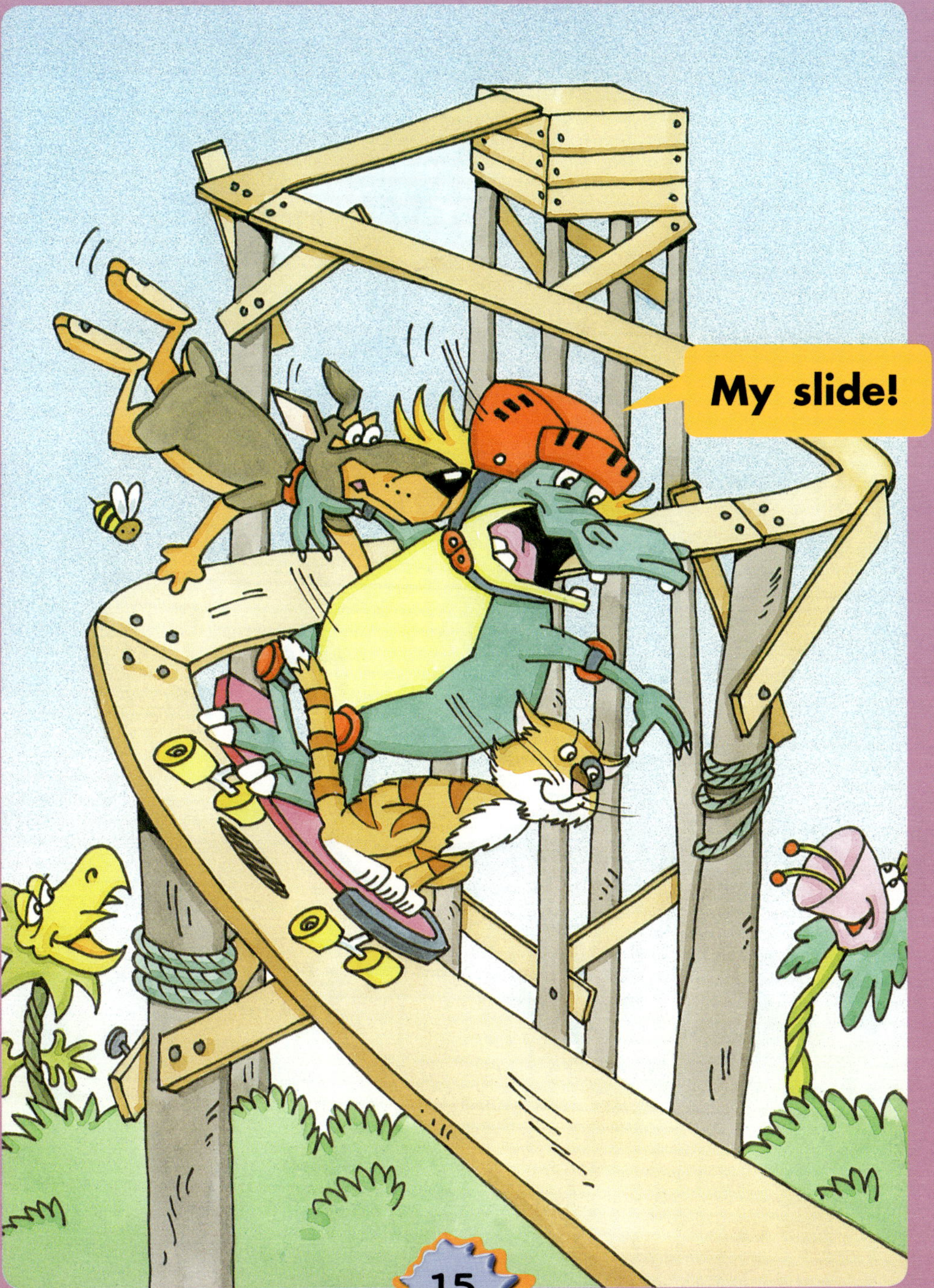
My slide!

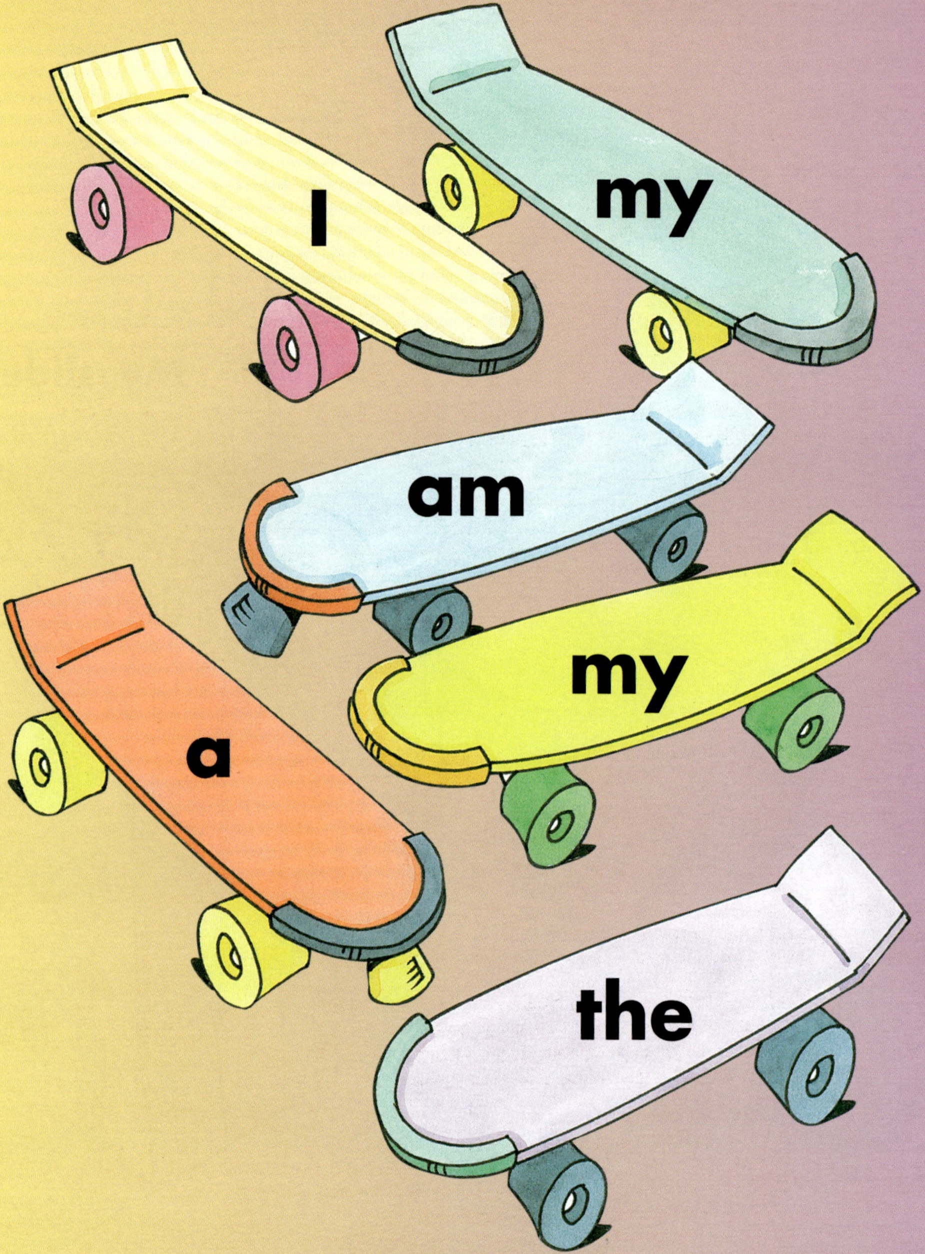
I
my
am
my
a
the